"My closet needs help," says Barbie. "It seems so messy. I really need to organize it."

"My closet, too," says Teresa. "My clothes are everywhere!"

"And my closet is such a mess I can't find my pink skirt," adds Nikki.

"I have a terrific idea," exclaims Barbie. "Let's help each other clean out our closets, and we'll donate some of our clothes to people who need them!"

"It's for a great cause," says Teresa. "The clothes are going to people who really need them."

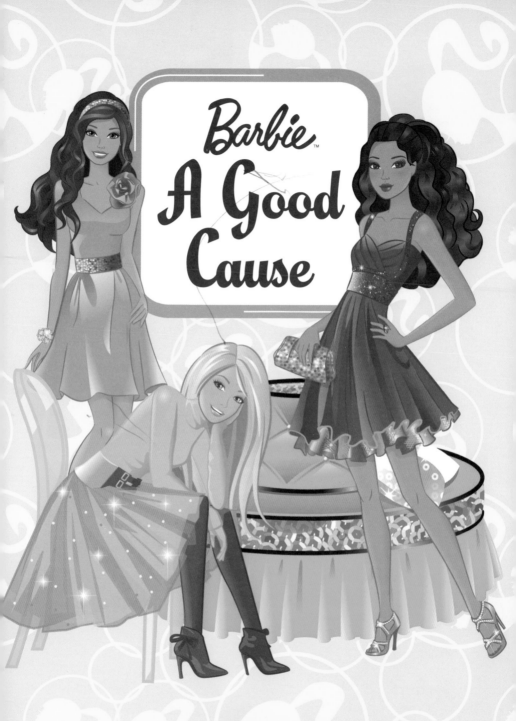

Barbie™
A Good Cause

Reader's
Digest
Children's Books®

New York, New York • Montréal, Québec • Bath, United Kingdom

Teresa and Nikki start sorting through their clothes while Barbie gives her opinion. Even Lacey wants to help!

"Let's try on everything. We want to make sure it all looks good," says Barbie.

"I love your feather skirt," says Barbie to Teresa.
"Your clutch looks great with my outfit," says Nikki.
"Hey, I have a great idea," says Barbie.

"Even when we wear each other's clothes, we do it in our own way. We should have a fashion show for the charity and show everyone that no matter what you're wearing, you can play with fashion to create your own style," Barbie says.

The girls strut down the runway. Barbie, Nikki, and Teresa each put their own unique spin on their outfits. The audience loves it.

The girls had a great time at the show, *and* helping the charity. And, of course, the newest trend in fashion is to borrow your friend's outfits and style it up your own way. All started by Barbie and her friends!

Check out the photos the girls uploaded.

How to Refresh Your Wardrobe

Accessorize! Look through your jewelry box (and ask to borrow from your mom, too) for necklaces, bracelets, earrings, and hair accessories.

With your parents' permission, exchange different clothes and accessories with your friends. And don't forget to match your outfit with a colorful purse!

Freshen up an ordinary outfit with cute shoes. Wear a pair of ballet flats with your skinny jeans and viola—a chic new look!

Design new fashions from what you already have in your closet! Invite your friends over to help you mix up the tops and bottoms you usually wear together to form a bunch of new outfits.

Ways You Can Help a Good Cause

1 Organize a bake sale where you donate all the profits to a charity of your choice!

2 Volunteer your time at a soup kitchen, nursing home, or any other organization that interests you.

3 Collect nonperishable groceries such as soup, cereal, canned veggies, etc. and donate them to a food pantry or a homeless shelter.